Broken Men

Sweet Edition

Mara Collins

Broken Men, Sweet Edition

Rights

Cover Art & Design: Mara Collins

Sweet Edition Issue, 2017

ISBN: 978-0997603330
ISBN-13: 099760333X

Contact Information including Rights & Publishing at www.LovingandLeaving.com

"Sometimes the horses don't come in the money"

Table of Contents

Broken Men

Rights

Part 1

1. 1

Jack

When Annie left the beard started growing and it didn't stop. Winter was coming and I didn't think it was worth shaving it. The days got colder. The house got darker each day, but the city of Minneapolis glowed brighter each night.

Annie said she liked the house, cause it reminded her of houses out home. Minneapolis wouldn't be so bad, cause it was just another island in the great wooded westward expansion. It was a quiet house, in a quiet-ish neighborhood, off a street named Minnehaha. But it needed help. I told her we'd clean it up more after the summer, in the fall, but she left and I had the house to myself.

"I'll get one of those community outreach clubs to come over and help you paint it. Maybe a fresh coat will do you some good. The kids love a good project." A colleague of mine suggested. I had gotten an adjunct teaching position at the law school, two classes that semester. It was a nice change. I needed to get out of Oregon.

So the kids came. And that is where I first met Kit. She was meek. Dark hair, pale skin. She wore a men's button-down, backwards as a smock over leggings and sneakers. She had large framed glasses, and she was put in charge of painting between the cabinets and the backsplash of the kitchen.

The head of the group, a gregarious blonde, managed the whole project seamlessly with a beaming smile. They showed up at 7 am and began to lay tarp over what little furniture I had.

"Just moved in," I grumbled hoping to shut down any questions.

"Well consider this our welcome to our great state." That girl said.

They were all so happy, painting, listening to music. To be 20...22 again. The future is all ahead of you.

I hardly even noticed Kit until I went to grab a beer, sit out in the backyard. Let them get their busy on. And there was Kit with a little dabbing pan and a sponge brush doing the kitchen in a soft gray. Her headphones were on. She looked over and stared at me solemnly, and I furrowed my brow and walked away. I didn't even know her name then.

The day progressed, my colleague came by and we chatted about an upcoming joint lecture. The student group took some pictures. That blonde girl organized a picnic lunch, and then back to work. Five o'clock rolled in and they all go in their cars, four or five of them to each of their beat-up old Volvos and Volkswagens and headed out.

The paint was even and clean. The rooms a crisp white or navy blue, I picked a bit arbitrarily based on the convivial recommendations given.

I went for a run and took a shower. Then at seven I came back to the kitchen and there she was finishing up the last corner.

"Hey Girl, your boat left," I said to her. She didn't look over. I was still in the habit of softly grumbling back then when I wasn't lecturing. I walked over and waved my hand, she took out a headphone.

"Sorry, do you need something over here."

"Yeah, uhh you know this whole thing ended a couple of hours ago."

She looked down at her brush and replied "Oh...I guess I didn't notice, well I uh...I will go catch the bus." She looked like the one passion she had in life was taken from her, as she began to close shop.

"Hey wait though...you can't uhh just leave with the one corner like that...can you uhh finish it? And then I can give you a ride back maybe."

Then she began to look frustrated. "I don't work for free. My time limit today was six hours. There is extra paint, you can finish it and I will take the bus....I need to go." Her face began to turn red, as she stuffed her bag quickly.

"Why don't I at least give you a ride at least. I didn't mean to take advantage of your, your generosity, I just thought that you stayed cause you enjoyed painting and..."

"A ride would be nice." She said looking down, a tear dropped down her cheek, I turned around trying to give her privacy. I felt absolutely terrible, and I had no idea what was wrong. But I tell you one thing, I couldn't be around another crying person then, cause I would start crying.

We got in my old pickup, and I began the drive down to the University.

"Listen I am sorry, I did not mean to assume you would uh work for free or anything," I said gruffly. The tears didn't explode, thank goodness, but her face was still red.

"No, no it's not you. I just thought someone would come and get me when it was time to leave. ...I am...I am 20 and sometimes I still feel like I am sixteen..."

"Life has a funny way like that." I just said.

"I joined the club to make friends. My parents said I'd feel pretty lousy if I went through college with no one new, no new experiences. But I just. I miss my friends, the people I am comfortable with"

"Don't just go doing things cause it makes your parents happy, if it is meant to be it's meant to be." I tried to give her some advice. Something vague. I hoped she wouldn't ask me anything.

"I guess."

"Listen if ugh you want to come back to finish it...seems like you liked the painting."

"I said you'd have to pay me." Her voice changed to sternness.

"Yeah, I could uh pay you. I have some other stuff that needs a uh discerning touch maybe you can help me with."

"I won't be your maid."

"That's not what I am saying, girl. I mean I have other rooms that need to be painted, paintings to be hung. I just moved in...."

"Well, I need the money."

"Hows about 8 dollars an hour," I said.

"Fine, when can I start?"

"Whenever's good for you." We pulled into campus. She directed me to her block of dorms, gave me her number, and she said she could do Wednesdays and Thursdays after 6.

"And what's your name?" I asked as she stepped out of my car.

"Kit."

"Kit what?"

"Just Kit." She said and walked away.

At first, I thought it wouldn't work out. I thought she'd wanna talk and not do anything, but quite the opposite. I'd give her a task, and she'd silently complete it.
I even paid her to give out Halloween candy as I graded papers.

She'd take the bus over, and I'd give her a ride home, and we honestly didn't talk much, just hellos and what did I need help with. By Thanksgiving every painting was hung, every item was unpacked, and I lived in my home. Most of the stuff I would buy and have shipped, wanting something a little new, a fresh me. I started to forget I ever had a before. I started to feel better.

The snow would come in the evenings, a light sprinkling, and every light was reflected 100 times over. Minneapolis was pretty like that. Even in the dark.

"So uh, what are you doing for Thanksgiving," I said a week before, on the drive home. I dunno what was in me, but I felt like making small talk.

"Going to my parents, they do a thing, gonna hang out with some friends."

"Oh sounds nice."

"Yeah I guess, it'll be nice to see everyone."

"So where is home?"

"St. Louis Park."

"Oh hey, that's right here."

"Yeah...em...what about you." She said, clearly deflecting the conversation away from herself.

"Just gonna stay home, get on some reading."

"Sounds relaxing." She said.

"Yeah may hang with friends too."

"How old are you?" She turned to me, bluntly.

"30, gonna be 31 in Feb," I said almost stupidly.

"You still count when you're gonna get older at 30?"

"30's not that old, 20."

"I'm 21." She replied.

"Oh uhh, you said..."

"My birthday was in October."

"Oh you never said anything."

"We're not much talkers, why would I tell you...you're my...boss I guess."

"Yeah I guess. Sorry, I didn't mean to intrude."

I dropped her off and as she exited the car, she said: "Stay young Jack." I laughed to myself and smiled. Then I stopped cause I realized I was smiling.

She didn't work that week, and I missed her. But it was different from when I missed Annie cause I didn't really miss Annie. She left, and I missed having her around, but I was angry. I was angry at her and I wanted her gone.

Then Kit called me the Sunday after Thanksgiving.

"Hey ugh, Jack...sorry Professor Nyquist."

"I guess I never said, but you can call me Jack," I replied.

"Yeah Jack, looks like your house is pretty together, and I want to thank you for all the work you have given me, but winter break is coming and I need more steady work so..."

A pang hit me, she was right. I didn't have much more for her to do. It did seem like she needed to money. She wore the same six shirts every time I saw her. Various blue button downs and leggings. Her sneakers had worn into the snow.

"What's your major," I asked, bluntly.

"Huh?"

"What's your major, Kit."

"I am in the Environmental Studies program." She replied.

"I have a need for a research assistant, do you want to help, I can pay you 9.25 an hour for that. It's through the break" It was made up. I made the whole thing up. But I did need help. I had a project on the back burner, for the land, for the will, and I needed to brush up on the Federal laws....I don't even know what I was feeling then. Just sure.

"What do you teach?" She replied.

"Environmental Law. Focused on land use and conservation, to the likes of that."

"Okay." She replied.

"I'll email you the details you, can come by next week, same time."

"Shouldn't we do this at your office?" She asked. I shared an office with an old, tenured constitutional law professor who was paid three times as me for teaching one class a term.

"Sure, I guess, if you have time during the day. That is until school ends, then the offices are closed" I tried to get out of it.

"I don't...so...six it will be."

After finals, when the school closed, she started coming in an old car, a beat-up Nissan.

"It's my father's he lent it to me for break." She said simply as I watched her from my front door. She was good at finding the articles, working quietly in my LexisNexis account sorting through cases on Federal land rights. I think she really thought they were for my class.

"So what are you doing for Christmas," I asked one day as we silently sipped tea, and highlighted important clauses in relevant contracts she had found.

"I uh...we're going to get Chinese food."

"Chinese food, is that some family tradition?"

"You could say that...I am Jewish, we eat Chinese food." She blurted out as if she had revealed something that she didn't like to share with people. I looked at her in the eyes, and I could see it. I could piece it all together almost, why she didn't fit in with the Nordic blondes and Englishman around her.

"Sounds like fun," I said gruffly and took a sip of my tea. She looked back down and began to go back from work. I wasn't really sure what to say next. I thought about saying, "Hey I know some Jewish people." But it sounded stupid. I did know a few guys from Law school, but in Astoria, there were no one except for us and our cousins by marriage, and we were all German or Irish or something like that. Things like that. Nyquist was a Swedish grandfather down the line. I didn't want to sound so unworldly. I could tell through the months, that she was quietly judging me, painting a picture. A sad old bachelor who dressed more like a lumberjack than a lawyer.

So I said, "This tea is shit, you want a beer?"

"I am not drinking with you." She shot back.

"Lighten up, Kit—a Leinenkugel or something?" I knew these Minnesotans loved their leinnies. She stopped a pondered for a moment.

"Sure." So I got up and got us a couple of beers, and we want back to work. But that only lasted for about five minutes, cause I wanted to know more about her and show here that I was something. I dunno why I wanted to prove myself to this girl, but I did. I wanted to be the person I wanted to be, and I thought was gonna start then.

"So you never told me, what's your last name."

"It's Cohen...and my full name is Akiva..."

"Akiva Cohen."

"You sound like such a goy when you say it, just stick to Kit."

"A goy?"

"A not Jewish person."

"Well, I'm not, I am from like Ireland or some Nordic Country...but really from Oregon."

"That's nice, are you enjoying Minnesota?"

"Yeah its nice, its a lot the same, a lot different."

"I've never been out that way, but I imagine I would like it. I like the trees and stuff, mountains." She flittered her hand around as though it was painting a picture.

So we talked about what Oregon was like, and I asked her why she seemed so miserable, and she laughed. She said she wasn't feeling miserable, so much. Her friends were home from school. She was the only one in her group that didn't leave the state, go to a school out east or something, and she was regretting it. We opened a second beer. She had gone to a local high school, a large one. Most of her friends she made at the temple or her Jewish summer camp. Minnesota was becoming isolating as everyone was leaving.

I didn't tell her about the land we had, or Annie. I just told her about the Pacific Northwest, going to law school in Seattle. How that was the biggest city I'd been in. She laughed. Her father was also a lawyer, but worked for a non-profit, as some sort of lobbyist, but in Environmental Law. His altruism prevented him from the real money-making positions. They traveled a lot for him to go to conferences. She'd been around America. She was born in Ithaca when her father was teaching at Cornell. Her parents were older. They moved out here for the lobbying position. We opened a third beer. I was really on my fourth.

She wanted to go to law school as well, and this assistantship was nice practice. I told her I could give her some recommendations. She said sure. She smiled. It was a very sincere smile. Not like she was trying to make me happy, but that at that moment she had a little moment of happiness. Like I gave her hope. I smiled, cause I had a little moment of happiness, too.

Then she said, she couldn't drive, and she needed to call a cab. I really wanted to ask her to stay. I had two extra bedrooms. Not cause I wanted to be with her, maybe I did then even. Maybe I just didn't want to be alone. Five beers was not a lot for me, but I dunno, I wanted to keep talking to her, or even sitting quietly looking at papers with her. And as the cab came and she got into it "if you don't mind I'll get the car in the morning."

As I lay in bed, I suddenly began to think about all the things I thought were odd before. The leggings, the shirts, the big glasses, the hair always in a sloppy bun that was falling down. I never liked the weird ones. Annie was just the opposite. Her shirts always stuck to her full breasts. Her hair, so fair. Annie was what a woman was, but Kit, well she had something that I took an interest in. I didn't do anything or nothing. I just was thinking about her.

She came to pick up the car the next day and said she'd see me after New Years.

1.2

Kit

When Soshi and Tova said we should go Uptown the day after Christmas for a girl's night, I knew they were planning something fun. I missed them so much. I fantasized about transferring; maybe there was a place for me in New York or Boston. But, I knew I was too far down the rabbit hole to transfer, and we had no money. I had no money. And I didn't want to have to take out more student loans. My parents struck a fear of those into me ("You can't absolve them if you were to go bankrupt!!---the rates constantly change no matter how good you are!').

It was a fear of unnecessary burden that drove my childhood. Only get involved if it is cheap and will lead you somewhere good. It seemed like a subversive frugality that many of my friends also lived by until High School. Then the have and have-nots became more apparent. But only to me. No one seemed to question the idea that I would stay in Minneapolis. Like they knew I'd always be here. Then they all left and came back. I was still in St. Louis Park.

We were at Hammer and Sickle, as Soshi gushed about NYU and Tova kept talking about her sorority at Washington University. From one St. Louis to another...Soshi had taken to wearing a gold watch that glimmered under the light. I had on my one pair of diamond earrings I got for my Bat Mitzvah. When anyone asked why I never got a new pair, I said because it was sentimental.

We ordered flights of Vodka and began to roll them back. I was the last one to turn 21, and it was a delight to finally have a night of us drinking outside of a basement. Soshi was Russian and she found the entire thing entertaining. Nastrovia with every glass hitting the back of the throat. "Ya have to make fun of these things...like the Producers and Hitler," Tova instructed... I laughed. Soon more people joined us from camp. My world was back. My little haverah.

We had all met somewhere between 6th and 7th grade. Some of us had gone to the same temple, but hadn't really spoken until a rafting trip at summer camp. By the fall, what had been an empty social calendar was filled with new Mitzvah invites. We stayed friends in High School. First kisses, first times. Many of us went to different schools, but we'd meet up at random coffee shops. I never wondered what their days were like before we met because I just assumed it started when we gathered. Our social lives were constructed around our insular group. My first kiss, my first heartbreak, my second kiss, my first best friend,.. We were in it together. Then, one day, we weren't. We were in different places, becoming different people. Or at least, everyone else was.

After we were perfectly happy and smashed, Josh convinced us to go do karaoke at a bar in the Warehouse District. Cuzzy's was famous and infamous. Anything goes, and it could turn into anything. The snow began to sprinkle, and as a post-Christmas celebration they had Karaoke in the cold.

Josh was at Georgetown, and it had chilled him out. His a-d-d turned into sharp focus and wit. He had hazel eyes and light brown hair and was probably considered a catch for those studious girls in D.C. His parents had already moved out of Minneapolis to Chicago. We rode in the cab together. He was sitting next to me, his friend in the front who he was staying with. His hand was already up my shirt slightly. I knew it, comfortably.

We didn't really start dabbling with each other till senior year. He was a late bloomer. After a family summer trip to Europe though, he was suddenly masculine, and worldly, and attracted to me. I was not a late bloomer, I had just never bloomed. I don't know why I ended up with him, but we all seemed to just couple up like that, at the end of every summer, and then it would reset somehow by June first. Senior year though was bliss. I had someone to text, to call, to spend time with other than Tova and Soshi. And I was weirdly comfortable with him, okay to explore. We had done a lot of exploring that year. No one was kidding themselves in our group about staying a virgin till marriage. It was more about being practical and realistic. Josh was my dose of realism.

"Kit, we never get time alone." He whispered in my ears. I nuzzled him gently on his chin. I always felt extra warm with him after a few drinks. We would never be together, like a couple, like we were. I knew that. I always knew that. But we were friends and when we took each other's virginities it was like we made a pact. Whenever he was in town, we'd try out our awkward, exploratory, fumbling sex.

When we got in I went to a corner, and he got me a beer. "Come out back." He pulled me away. Soshi gave me a wink. His arm was around my waist as we laughed our way into a corner slinking around people. A drunk guy on the stage singing.

"Kit." A gruff voice called out. I looked over my shoulder. There was Jack Nyquist, flanked by some friends. He raised his beer to me, and for some reason, I raised mine to him. I'd never seen him out, but I was unsurprised by his choice of companionship. Two more men in plaid shirts, holding their beers with their arms in perfect angles.

Josh pulled me deeper to the side of the stage. The night was flying .We began kissing. Our lips cold and chapped with each exchange. Josh barely noticed the that I had spoken to someone other than him.

Then I heard the gruff voice on the stage. A little louder, a little clearer than its normal grumble.

"This is uh, I guess for a girl I met out here. It's been quite a year, but hell it's been good to have her." I stopped kissing and looked up on the stage.

"Look at that guy, god I miss Minnesota." Josh laughed, and coolly took a final
sip of a beer.

Then he proceeded to sing "Start me Up". I couldn't take my eyes off him, honestly. He got into the song, and suddenly his grump became almost a deep singing voice.

"That's was a dare, I know, I am terrible, thank you, And Kit I love you. Thank you, Minneapolis"

My face turned red. Was he talking to me? What other Kit did he know? But it was cold and Josh couldn't see, so I turned around and began to kiss him again.

1.3

Jack

"Whose Kit?" Jason asked me.

"Ahh, friend of mine, saw in the crowd. Wanted to give a shout out."

"Brother, it's good to see you having fun."

"Jase seeing you is just what I needed."

We crashed at my house. It must have been about 2 in the morning when we got in the door.

The next morning, the hangover was something like in my 20s. Jase walked into my room, shirtless, in some sweat pants. We both still slept the same way. It was like we were still in high school, rising early to hunt. My brother would always be my brother.

"There's some chick sitting outside your house in a beat up car, dude. Got a little creeped, so I had to cut my run short."

He was only a year younger, but he was a bigger guy, in those slight ways. His height, just a little, his arms, just a little. But in other ways, I was bigger. I had more of a trail, more in my past. He stayed home, I left. I was the one with a wife, then I guess an ex-wife. I owned houses, and I was one who had the burden to figure out what would happen to the family business. He just managed it. But I think we loved our roles, we loved our place. It was symbiotic, it gave us a way to define ourselves.

He worked in the woods, the foreman. All the extra muscle and hair kept him warm. I knew it served a purpose. But sometimes, I was jealous of my brother. Not that I didn't work out every week. But I couldn't keep more than 20 pounds of muscle on me. I had to remember I was in an office. I didn't need to be barreling like the rest of the guys in Astoria. For a moment, before he responded, I looked forward to him going back to Oregon. I liked me being without family, again. I liked not having to explain things, to solve problems.

I stood up and looked out my bedroom window. It was Kit, she was moving her hands a bit, looked like she was talking to herself. My mind flashed back to Cuzzy's, which was a friend of Jase's from college's idea. He'd never been to Minneapolis, but he still knew two guys there and their friend who were willing to help his younger brother cheer up. He was that guy.

I suddenly got in a panic and ran downstairs and out the front door, across the street to her car. She looked up and then rolled down her window. I put my hands on her car to steady myself. It was like it was happening all over again, but differently this time. It wasn't in the middle of the night. It was the day. She was still there, she was waiting for me, I had a chance. The sky was gray. The ground was white, even the pavement was white from the brine fighting the ice.

"I thought the other guy was crazy for running shirtless in 30-degree weather but now you're shirtless and barefoot as well."

"It's my brother. I uh." The cold hit my feet first, then my chest. I stopped for a second, trying to collect myself. "Can I come in the car?" I said, more calmly.

She unlocked the passenger side door with her arm and I ran around the outside. I sat down and she turned up the heat and grabbed a blanket from the back seat and wrapped it around my shoulders.

Then she sat quietly looking forward down the street.

"I...umm, I feel like however this conversation goes it's not gonna be good for anyone, or feel good..."

I turned my head to her. Her face was red. But I knew, this time, she was embarrassed.

And I did something; I never even did with Annie. I put my hand on her shoulder and began to brush her hair out of her face. She turned to me. It was like lightning or something was running through my arm or something.

"Whatever you said last night, whatever....Whatever you saw with me and that guy...I don't think anyone noticed any of it...I don't think it mattered. I just need to know if I can keep my job, now...cause I need to money for school and stuff...and if I have to start looking again..." She just started quietly saying, as her eyes moved down not meeting me in the eye.

I wanted to say to her, *"I'm a broken man, and I say things, and I do stupid shit. Men do stupid shit. And I do, I do care about you. You are the only steady thing I have right now, and that's pretty fucked up. And I didn't mean to break this..."*

But I knew what she wanted to hear. She wanted it all to go away. I put my arm back under the blanket and said "Yes, of course. I was drunk, and I was trying to express...it was nice to see you having fun.... you don't seem like you do a lot of that...or enough of it."

"I was drunk, too. Thank you for understanding." Then she looked up at me, and for once in the light of day I really saw her. Outside the dark of my house or the dusky drives home. Her hair was five thousand types of brown glimmer. Her eyes, dark so that you couldn't tell the pupil from the iris. Like god made her to hold secrets.

"I am...I will see you in January." I let out.
"See you in January." She said. I pulled off the blanket and began the cold walk back to my front door.

I am a broken man, and I was intermingling with this young lady, who still had time to come out intact. I needed to stop.

1.4

Kit

I came back on January 2nd like I said would happen and we went back to the quiet review until it was just me reviewing for as he began to prep for his spring classes. He seemed quieter, more removed than ever. And I found myself staring at him. His red beard, his rust-colored hair, his blue eyes. The way his shirts lightly clung to his arms. He seemed so typical and yet interesting.

I had sometimes thought back to that morning a few weeks earlier. I probably could have just pretended I didn't hear him, or his actions were meaningless. But I woke up and thought, something had happened and I needed to address it head on. It was going to be a New Year and I wasn't going to be passive. Things weren't just going to happen to me anymore, I was going to control them.

Josh had one more week in Minneapolis before heading to his parents and then back to school. We were furious when we could get two seconds alone. It was a comfortable feeling inside me. His quick releases. His fingers finishing me. His ability to try anything. I felt almost proud, I owned my own coming to with him. My parents were right, I needed to try new things explore more outside of my inner circle.

After that morning, I felt like I had a certain confidence, to be more direct with Jack. Like I had some upper hand. I told him when I found a new link to an article that needed to be reviewed. He was interested in land rights granted by the Federal government for various agricultural practices. How it passed in a family or company, when it didn't pass on. What it meant to be stewards of the land.

February came, and then March, and suddenly through the quiet hush of every Minneapolis winter came the hope of a long spring and a fleeting summer.

"So you going home for Spring Break?" I finally blurted one day, when I had enough of the silence, of his fear of me.

"No, I don't really need to."

"Oh..."

He sat the papers he was grading down and said without looking up. "My brother comes out here when I need family...but I think I like Minneapolis."

"Really, how would you know, you don't seem to go out much." I blurted.

"I do things when you're not here..."

"Really?"

"And its winter, its cold."

"That's the best time."

"Maybe when it's spring." The conversation seemed to slow, so I said

"What's it like to have a twin brother."

"He's not my twin..."

"Oh it's just that....you guys look so alike."

"I think it's the beards..."

"No I mean you have pretty much the same body." And then he looked up and I looked down. I could feel my cheeks getting flush. For a second, from the corner of my eye, it looked like he smiled a little.

"We're only a year apart, maybe that's it..."

"Yes maybe..." I said quickly, highlighting absolutely nothing on a blank page to look busy.

"You got siblings, Kit?"

"No, just me."

"I got a sister too, Becky. But her husband's in the fishing and shipping industry. So she tends to be an outsider...you know cause we're land people."

"Land people?"

"Yeah we got some land in Oregon...logging land." I scrunched my face a little. It seemed weird an environmental lawyer would come from a logging family.

"I know what you thinking." He said and put down his paper and leaned back on his chair. "But the land, it's mostly unlivable. And the forest, it regrows two, three times a generation. We don't cut it that often, and it gives this place for the animals. The life of a tree can be like any other animal. It's as long or as short as nature allows. It has youth, adulthood, it's old age. t It's a balance, cause we need the forest, but the forest needs us."

I looked up at him, for some weird logic it made sense. He looked me dead in the eye, and for a moment I felt it. I felt a tension, to want something then and there, and not be able to reach and get it. But this time, it was actually something I wanted. I never wanted to fit in outside of my group, my friends. I had them, and they had me, and in this moment it didn't matter. We had our own Minneapolis. But, I suddenly wanted to know what it was like to touch him, his rough freckled skin. And I thought...I could of probably tried that morning, in December. But it was weird seeing him so vulnerable. Like I would have been taking advantage of him. And then I wouldn't have had the job. The perfect job for a resume to law school....I'd be done with school in December of that year, which gave me plenty of time to prep applications...get into a great school...I knew I just needed to get through it.

I'd never had that before. Josh was the crème of the crop at camp, and even as we grew into adulthood. I always had him.

"I gotta finish this one paper," I said to change the subject.

"Right." He replied. And we went back to work.

1.5

Jack

April was wet, and cold, but like home cold. The cold of the water, pushing air back onto you. So I kept the beard. We would talk every now and again, about my class or the research. She began to piece together I was looking for legislation that may pertain partially to the family land. She didn't seem to mind.

We went back to doing some outdoor chores. Planting bulbs in the lawn, seeding it with grass. She began to make more sense to me. She had some sort of penny-pinching practicality about her. She was focused and had a goal. And yet she seemed to admire me. Listen to what I said. And she had no idea, that I had the whole other life, that I was this whole other person. I was beginning to absorb new pieces she seeded in me. Around her, I enjoyed it. It was like, I was this new self.

I thought of her at night, about what her plans were, what she might do with her life. She told me she had a few friends from camp, that were going to school out of state, and an on again off again boyfriend. Probably the guy she was kissing that night at the bar. He went to school at Georgetown and was graduating in the spring. I began to wonder about her, whether she did more than kissing with him. About how I would kiss her. I would catch her from time to time, staring at me. And I felt a little bashful and a little proud. She was too smart for a guy like me. She was so worldly. She knew these kinds of people who would leave and come back to her. I had my brother and a family burden.

Then it was almost May, and there were only a few weeks left in the semester. And she asked if it was okay if she stopped working for the summer. She said she had plans. And my heart sank. And suddenly it was like I had this clock in my head, that I needed to do something before she was gone before I was gone. I did not know if they would even renew my contract for the next year.

It just happened. But it was terrible and I failed her miserably.

It was a bright morning and we were outside clearing the back lawn. I asked if she wanted a beer or something. We hadn't drunk together really since that night in the fall. She said sure and we got to work. She was wearing her smock shirt, that backwards men shirt. We began to plant beds of field flowers that would grow tall through the summer. It was her idea. She said everyone did it.

I was trying to help her hold the bag of topsoil as she spread it when I lost the grip and it spilled all over her. Her hair, her shirt, her shoes.

"I'm sorry, Kit...let me ugh get you a change of clothes...let me just go look...One second..." She sat out there in the wet soil and drank her beer. She was laughing about the whole thing as she began to pull dirt out of her hair and tried to wipe her glasses. I found an old pair of sweatpants and a tee shirt and handed them to her.

"We can, uh, finish this another day."

"Do you mind if I take a rinse, I have soil....in my hair and stuff."

"Yes, yes of course." I let her use my bathroom, as the guest one didn't even have towels. I never had guests.

I went downstairs and had a shot of vodka. I was embarrassed, how unprepared I was. I could hear the shower turn on, and the shifting of the floor beams. I thought how I only had generic shampoo in there, and a bar of old soap. Then I heard the shower turn off, and remembered I didn't even put out a towel for her. A few moments later I heard her walking downstairs. I didn't even know what to do, so I reached for two more beers and opened them. I was standing with both of them in my hands, probably pale as a ghost, as she walked into the room. Her hair long and wet, soaking through the tee shirt. She wasn't wearing the sweatpants I gave her. Just her bare legs and feet touching the kitchen floor. I looked down and put out one arm, almost shoving, saying "Beer?"

She took it, and took a sip, and said "You pants are too big...I uh...I threw my stuff in the laundry if you can show me how to turn it on..."

"Yeah sure." I kept my eyes down as I followed her to the staircase. But as she walked in front of me up, the stairs, I could see the bottom of her slipping from under my shirt. I wanted to reach out and grab it, to touch her. But I looked down again. I fumbled with the machine, turning it on for her.

"I can uh wait here..."

"It's gonna be at least an hour," I said, still darting my eyes between her face and the floor.

"Oh yeah...I uh...I am a little drunk, though...I need to take a nap before I go home... or call a cab..."

"You can use the guest room," I said and pointed to the door.

"Sure." She said. I looked up, and could see was also staring down at her feet. Her face as flush, and she was tugging at the bottom of the shirt.

"You are beautiful," I said, almost unintelligibly. I just blurted it out, so badly wanting her to look up, to own herself.

"What?" She said quietly and look at me. I could see her hair was drying into loose waves on her shoulder, her legs milky and soft. Her breasts left a silhouette under the cotton.

Then I put down my beer and scooped my arm around her and kissed her. She fell to the floor, and I on top of her. I looked at her, afraid maybe I was too forward. Did I break her? Maybe this was too much. But she looked back at me and wrapped her leg around me and began to kiss me back. I pulled us up and carried her to the guest bedroom. Her legs wrapped around my waist. When my hand was holding the bottom of her back I realized she wasn't wearing underwear....must have been that way the whole time. Maybe she wanted this...or maybe, I don't know. I knew by then I didn't really know woman the way I thought I did...or maybe I hadn't ever at all.

I stopped and I looked at her and asked, "Is this okay?"

She looked at me, without her glasses, her expression so stern. "If something happens that isn't, I'll let you know...This is okay"

And so I started kissing her neck slowly, and she arched her back as I pulled my shirt off her bare chest. I laid her on her back, on the bed and began to take my shirt off.

Her eyes were unreadable. But fixed on me. I let my hand graze her down her stomach. My finger moving between her chest down below and I stopped for a second. And I realized how beautiful she was, and how pure she was, and what was going to happen next...would I really never see her again? Was this just the climax after Annie leaving me? And I began to feel profoundly sad. Kit deserved better. She didn't need to be broken by me.

Then she began to pull my pants down. I grabbed her hand. And I pulled her close till she was hugging me, and I whispered in her ear. "I can't do this."

"Yes, you can...it's okay." She said back. And began to kiss my neck and then I pulled away. And got off the bed.
"No ...I mean..."
"What's wrong," she said, suddenly relaxing into the bed,
"I just...I am...I can't be with you..." I looked down at her.
It took a moment for her to register what I said. Then, she pulled her knees in front of her, trying to hide. And I could fee for the first time since Annie left, the tears coming back to my face. I pretended to clear my throat and looked down, pulling my pants back up. Holding them back.
I went to the hallway and grabbed the shirt and brought it to her, but her face, normally so calm or flustered, just looked so intent. She stood up,
"No, you don't get to do this." She pushed the shirt out of my hand and strode to the washing machine, where she pulled her clothes, wet but wrung.
"Kit, please take some warm clothes..."
"No, I am okay."
"Stay please let me...I just."

She held them in a bundle naked in my hallway. She began to put them on, and I tried to stop her...maybe if I could stop her she would stay we could figure this out. Whatever that was.

"You've had too much to drink, I've had too much to drink," I said trying to diffuse something I had royally messed up.

She just looked at me, then she darted down my stairs. Still undressed. Then in my foyer, she began to pull open the ball of clothes.

"Kit, I love you...I meant it...I mean it...I just am a broken man. A fallen tree who had no purpose. And you, you are young, you deserve better..."

"I just need to find my shirt and get dressed and then I will go, don't worry..."

"You have your whole life ahead of you, you are just a girl."

She found her shirt and stopped looking at me.

"What the fuck are you saying." She put her shirt on.

"You are still young, and being with me..." I tried to explain.

"You're broken, I get it. You'll break me...because our sex would be so mind shattering that I would constantly think about you with every guy I am with next?" She laughed and shook her head as she put on her leggings. "Or is it that your sex is so powerful it would break my vagina. Newsflash Jack, not a virgin, highly sexually active. I don't break that easily."

"No that's not what I am saying...don't say that..."

"Oh it's cause I look so pure, you don't wanna ruin that..."

She put on her shoes and opened the door.

"Fuck you. Fuck you. Fuck you." She ran out slamming the door behind her. She was gone before I could even gather what I wanted to say to her. I wanted to say, *I was the broken one. The one with the wife who was god knows where. With the family in a subtle, passive-aggressive land-feud. With no real job looking forward.*

Part 2

2.1

Kit

My dad took me to Ithaca for a month before summer sessions started, and it really was like something out of Dirty Dancing. He was attending a seminar series at Cornell and I spent my days at coffee shops downtown, and nights at Ithaca's finest ivy establishments. It was Townies and summer semester geeks who didn't want to go home. I met a kid, Christopher. About to be a sophomore. My dad said he was nice, and I was in his room in a house he rented with a few friends who were already gone, riding him, for a week before I left to come home.

It was like a real fuck you, to the last school year. I had been holding onto who I was from High School throughout the first three years of college, and it was not serving me well. I needed to be a new person. Or at least a different one. I ended up moving in with my parents and not renewing the dorm since I only had till the end of the year left. But being back there was different than high school. There was no curfew, and Soshi and Tova were free to come whenever they wanted. For once my liberal parents were actually acting what they had professed all these years. I had enough money saved to live a sparsely fun time.

I told them about Christopher. Not about Jack. But I also said I was looking to try something new other than Josh this summer or at least when he wasn't there. Josh was spending the summer with his parents but was planning to come by for a few weeks in July. Soshi was going to take my intro to Environmental Law class with me this summer, claiming that if she wasn't in a class her parents would make her work. This was the new Kit, same friends, just one with more confidence, more of a goal. I was going to finish my degree. I was going to go to law school. It was all going to happen for me.

"Says there was a professor change." Sosh read on the emailed syllabus.

"Whatever these summer classes tend to be a breeze." I laughed. We'd been planning all week what we'd wear and where we would hang out before and afterwards. I had never had a class with a friend before. I had never gone to school with a friend before.

We took our seats in the auditorium. It was one of the old-fashioned lecture halls which made Sosh giggle since she was so used to the new wave NYU classrooms.

"How are you suppose to know your competition if you can only see the back of their heads." She laughed.

"Don't worry this is a state school."

Then the door opened and a man in a dress shirt and slacks came in. He was wearing glasses and had rust-colored hair. He put his leather messenger bag down and looked up in the audience. It was Jack. But a different Jack. A professional Jack. The beard was gone, and I could see he had strong bone structure. His shirt was clean pressed and tucked in. He looked almost dashing. I began to shrink in my seat. Good thing we were far up, as Sosh had said "We need some privacy." Little did she know.

"Welcome to Intro to Environmental Law, I am your new professor, Jack Nyquist. You can call me Professor Nyquist." He started lecturing, sort of walking around the floor like it was a stage, not really looking up or at anything.

"Sorry, your old professor needed to take a last minute sabbatical. But do not worry, I think I have the right credentials for this. So a bit about myself, then roll call, then the syllabus, and then that's all I think for today..."

He wasn't the brusk, grumbling awkward guy I remembered. His voice was the same, it was still deep, and a bit twangy, but he seemed sure in his words, like this was what he was meant to do.

"I am an Environmental Lawyer by practice, undergrad University of Oregon, JD at U-Dub. I practiced first for the state of Oregon, but I thought I needed to branch out so after that I was practicing in Washington for private firms and lobby groups, mostly in agriculture, lots in the wine industry, beer inadvertently with the hops, alcoholic plantings in general...good stuff... Fun I know. Then I moved into teaching at the University of Washington while working for my families logging company, before coming here. I think my passion is sustainable enterprise, and I can't wait to learn about yours. So onto roll call...."

There were only 20 kids in the class, most of them in my program of environmental studies, and a few pre-law. It was a breezer for the prelaw kids, and for us it was a tortuous undertaking. For them this was the basic, for us this was the thing holding us back for making a difference.

"Shoshana Abramson." He started. I hoped there were a lot of people between A and C. There usually were in Minnesota.

"Here." She called out, and then turned to me. "Handsome goy, I think I've seen him somewhere."

"Kit Cohen." He said briskly and for the first time looked up to scan the classroom.

"Here." I chirped, raising my hand slightly, before falling back into my seat.

"That's so awesome that you can register by nicknames here. At NYU they don't let you and all the Chinese kids spend the first day telling the professors they'd rather be called Ben than Cheng." I laughed a little, trying to go with it. But no, I was Akiva Cohen on the roll sheet and I knew it.

He kept going without missing a beat, going over the syllabus and then a quick theoretical lecture on the history of Environmental Law in the world. Homework was some readings on the founding of the United States and earlier Environmental Laws, with a paper outlining three major earlier statues of our findings.

When he was done he went to his messenger bag and began to shuffle pages and Soshi and I descended down the stairs arm in arm.

"This is so much fun." She squealed, pulling my arm. And as we walked out I looked over my shoulder and he looked at me, and I could tell he knew I wanted to say, *"Don't acknowledge anything."*

2.2

Jack

I kept my cool. I didn't let anything phase me, I never do. I kept my cool because after she left that day, and I let myself cry. I realized I was happy. I didn't miss Annie anymore. I wanted other people. I was really free. I called up Jase and told him about it and he seemed happy for me. I didn't tell him how I knew Kit, but just that I was over Annie. I wasn't going back to Oregon, I liked Minneapolis, but I needed to get out, do stuff. He called up his old friend, Jeff and before you know it I was at a baseball game with some great guys. I met a nice enough woman,, we exchanged numbers and went on a date.

Then the school called. The undergraduate professor in Environmental Law had a death in the family and needed the summer off. I had a job, for at least another six weeks. I thought, this summer, I was gonna give it my A game. I was gonna shave my beard and show up dressed more like a professor and less like a mountain man. And I did.

I showed up to that first day of class ready to go, the sea of faces un-phasing me, and then I got to roll call. I read her name first, but I didn't want to say Akiva. It just came out as Kit. And I looked up. I heard her voice, a high pitched yes or something in the back row. I could barely see her and that was good. Because I just went back to the list. I saw her as she left class with her friend. I had never seen her with her friends, outside of that one night. She seemed happy. I did not want to disturb her. So I let her go.

But then I got home. I took off my shirt and went for a run. When I got home four hours later it was dark. I didn't know what to do. I didn't know what to do until I got her paper the next week. It was well written. Her choices a bit esoteric, but thoughtful. I wrote so on the paper. Made some recommendations for other statues that were more relevant. She earned her A-. But on the last page, I put a sticky note that said, *let's chat about this.* Inconspicuous.

I could have let the entire summer go on with just her showing up sitting in the back row, giggling with her friends. But a part of me, couldn't let her go.

I had a second date with the nice enough woman that night before the following class. And she came home with me, and I slept with her, in the guest room. I didn't want her in my bedroom. I didn't want her getting to know me, and she didn't seem to want to. She was out before the end of the night.

The next day I was well rested, and I handed back the papers. Went on with my lecture and gave out the next assignment. It was a Monday-Wednesday class. It was Monday, so I would see her again Wednesday.

But when she didn't reach out to me before Wednesday I became nervous. It was on Friday afternoon when I saw her standing leaning on the side of her beaten up car looking at my front door...I opened it up and looked down at her, not sure what to do next. It was a jolt back, to a person I had only visited before, and with her. The unsure person, the person who didn't have all the answers. It was like when I saw her, she erased all the practiced tricks and tools I had written in my book.

She was dressed differently than her usual look. Black shorts, a loose gray tee-shirt and a leather saddle bag with sandals. Her normal frames had been replaced with oversized sunglasses. As if the 60-degree day was the hottest she'd ever experienced.

"You should put a shirt on." She called from across the street, waving.

"I...uh, wanna come in," I said.

She began to walk over, I looked at the mess in the living room for a shirt frantically.

"This place is a mess." She announced as she closed the door behind her. "It's fine about the shirt." She laughed a little.

"I wanted to...talk to you about your paper."

"No, you didn't." She said assuredly. It was weird, she had been gone for almost two months, and yet it seemed like it had been years.

"No, I didn't," I replied.

"You wanted to check in make sure of...I dunno...You know I am not crazy Jack. I am not gonna blow this class of because whatever happened between us." She waved her hand between us, because she also knew, I think, it was hard to explain. "I have just the fall semester left, then I am free. I can head to law school. You want to keep your job....Don't worry....This isn't going to spiral out of control." She sounded assured.

"I want to make sure you are okay, too...I think." I said. Scratching the back of my head. I could see she had lost her timid nature around me. Now it just Kit, letting herself be.

"I'm okay. Are you okay?"

"I am okay," I said.

"Stand up straight, and stop fidgeting. You're like the most virile, nordic man I've ever seen anywhere near naked in person... You should enjoy your virility." I stood up straight and laughed.

"I mean..."

"I didn't even get your pants all the way off, take a compliment." She laughed. I walked over to her, and gave her a hug, she held me back. Burrowing her head into my chest. I could smell her hair, like warm oranges.

She pulled away.

"Let's, uh, put something on the calendar for August when this is done. Lunch or something."

"I'll send you an email," I replied. And she let herself out. And the rest of the term I was her professor lecturing, taking questions and she handed in her homework and it was nice. Simple. I went on a few more dates, a few more nights in bed with the woman, her name was Whitney.

I didn't email her, though, I called her and started talking before she even had a chance to say hello. I don't even know what I was thinking, but I was happy and I wanted to share it with her.

"Come celebrate with me, they picked up my contract for another year. Two classes in the fall, two in the spring."

"Oh wow, okay sure...where do you wanna go."

"My friends are going to a campground for the weekend, come with me." I don't know why I didn't invite Whitney, it would have probably been the more appropriate choice...Jeff just said he was getting a few houses by a lake, I told him I was bringing someone. I wanted to spend time with Kit.

"Sure, when are we leaving." She replied.

So on a Thursday afternoon she met me at my place with two bags (her stuff, and camp gear I might have forgot...I told her we knew how to camp in Oregon) and we piled into my pickup and headed out. We headed north to a small lake east of Big Fork. She spent most the time navigating us, and we swapped camp stories. She from her Jewish camp, me from hunting with my brother out along the hills above the Columbia River.

Jeff was already there "That's your cabin, man. Feel free the freshen up or whatever you need to do" He said with a wink and pointed to a log structure with large mesh windows at the end of the row. There was a bathroom inside, but the shower was on the outside.

"I uh, hope you don't mind, we may have to share a bed, but I brought my own sleeping bag..." I said as we went in.

She closed the door behind me.

"Good we're here and now I have you trapped. " She closed the door behind her and laughed.

She was wearing a flowery summer dress. She closed the curtains.

"Are you sure you wanna do that, it's gonna get hot in here," I called as I began to unpack my bag. But when I looked over, saw that she was slipping the dress off over her head.

"Do you ever wear underwear?" Was the first thing I said. It just felt so natural, she felt so natural there.

She laughed and said, "I barely have any boobs, I don't need to." She walked over to me, and we began kissing... it was as if what had happened, how I had treated her, she forgot. She pulled me over to the bed and I pulled up my shirt over my head. She held me closer. I could feel her tiny mounds against my chest. She brushed her hand through my hair and then down until she was unbuttoning my jeans.

"Hold on," I said and reached for a condom. She was now turned around kneeling. I put my hand between her cheeks and down, feeling inside her wet folds.

"Don't tease me." She said, but then I tried to turn her around on her back. I wanted to see her. I wanted to kiss her every inch, to watch her come.

"We don't have to do it missionary," she whispered as I leaned down, about to put myself in her.

"I want to start like this." I whispered back, "I want to make love to you."

"Who knew you were a romantic." She said.

"You did," I replied, and suddenly I stared down at her, and it began to happen again. But this time, it was different. She wasn't this pure creamy creature shuddering at my touch.

When it was over, I pulled out and threw the condom in the dustbin. She lay on the bed, her hand under her breast. I lay down next to her, and she looked at me, she sat up a little, and then looked down. Her face becoming a little flush. And the urge to hold her came over me and I pulled her close.

2.3

Kit

I don't know why I agreed to go into the woods with him or his friends, but the entire ride all I could think about is how I just needed to be with him, so I... so we... could get over what happened in the spring. And we were together. And it was creamy and plain but fulfilling, but too deep. I secretly wanted him to just plunge into me, to be the man I had built him up to be. It took him a while, in the end, it happened.

But then I felt embarrassed. Maybe I had pushed him too hard to do this. We got dressed in swimsuits and spent the rest of the afternoon with his friends diving in the lake. That night there was a fire and we made tacos while drinking beers.

And I fell asleep in the crook of his arm. And the next morning we had sweet sex again. And it was creamy and plain. It made me miss Josh a bit. Josh was always willing to try a new move or position. It was like we were friends practicing for future lovers. Maybe it was the campground and the less than privacy around us.

On Sunday we drove home, and I asked if I could take one last shower at his place before I returned to my parents. He obliged. I began to run the water, naked in the white tiled room, and I thought I had an extra day of clothes...maybe if we were home it could be something more satisfying.

So I walked downstairs naked. He was there in his boxers drinking a beer, poking around in the fridge.

He looked up, "What's this?"

I grabbed his hand and he raced me up to the shower, where we both got inside. I began to kiss him, pull him close. But I could feel him hesitating.

"Why don't we just take a shower."

"Sure" I smiled meekly. He pulled out the soap and began to lather my back.

"Let's just enjoy these moments..."

"Before we have to go back to reality."

"Yeah."

The water washed over us. When we were done cleaning up, we turn the water off and he found me a fresh towel.

"I guess I'll go," I said after I got dressed.

"It seems like there is something wrong Kit...."

"I, I dunno...nothing...I was just hoping..."

"We can still be together through the fall...we can still have us..."

"No, I just..." And then I said it. I said the thing that was in the back of my mind most of the weekend. He had projected on to me this persona, that just was not me...

"This was fun, but let's leave it at this weekend..."

"Why, we're not going to be in the same school..." He said pulling my close. I pulled away.

"No, that's not the problem," I said.

"What is it...is it about what happened in the spring...I thought everything was okay now..."

"Kinda, but I don't think it's okay."

"What is it?"

"I think you put me on a pedestal or something...I can't explain it, but I can feel it...I can feel it when we try to, be together, even when we accomplish it...it's like you're afraid to hurt me...like I am some clean creature that you can take only

47

a bit of pleasure in...like you're afraid to damage me...In the process, you might actually be damaging me more"

We were in his foyer and he looked down.

"I don't know what to say..." He said simply.

"For months I watched you, and I thought maybe he...maybe this man can satisfy me...maybe I was projecting...maybe I was hoping you were something you weren't...and then that thing happened...and you accused me of...not being a woman...being a girl...even though you know nothing about me...and I guess I know nothing about you...but when I want to...to get fucked like a woman...it's like you don't want to be that man."

He looked up at me and looked me in the eyes, and a sudden concern came over his face.

"I don't know you, and...you don't know me...You are probably the sixth woman I have been with...did you know that...The first I tried to be with after my wife..."

"You're married?"

"She's gone. I just...I thought you were the right person to become this better person with....but you are right....I was just projecting onto you."

I felt terrible, his face so solemn, as if he was suddenly faced with his own mortality. And he was married...I wanted to cry, but I didn't want him to see me cry. I didn't want to deal with this problem when I had bigger things to worry about. My future... my goals....So I grabbed my stuff and ran out the front door and went home.

2.4

Jack

The cleaner clothes stayed, but the beard came back. More trim this time, out of a matter of some practicality to protect my face against the cold whipping winds.

She was right. I felt terrible. Our friendship, our relationship, whatever it was, was superficial. She was like this bird who I enjoyed watching, but couldn't be with. I didn't even know the type of being with she wanted. I hadn't been with someone so intently since the first years with during law school Annie.

Annie idolized me throughout high school. She was a grade below me, with my sister. She'd be there out the kitchen counter, as my brother and I would come in from hunting deer with my father. She dated Jase briefly. It was childish, he was only sixteen, she was fourteen. He said they never even kissed. The only person that even knew was Becky, our sister. But everyone knew when we got together my senior year. We were all a year older...I was planning to leave for school, anyhow, and it just felt like something that should be done.

I remember it being awkward...the first time we had sex. We told each other, or really she told me she wanted me to be her first. I was young and I took it. And then I went to college, and I didn't see her for a while. I had another girlfriend during that time, we'd go to football games and out with friends. I joined a fraternity and she was in a nearby sorority. When college was over we parted ways easily.

It wasn't until law school. I was hanging out with some people I knew in Seattle, I must have been about 26, entering my last year, when I ran into her at some divey club in Belltown. It had been almost seven years since I saw her.

She had changed. Boy, she had changed. She had always had breasts, but now they were sizeable, and she owned them, and she was confident. Her blonde hair seemed brighter, her blue eyes fuller. She was in her last year at Seattle Pacific. We began to hang out. Then we began to sleep together, but that second time around it was less awkward and more fun. But she was this good girl at heart. She went to a Christian school. So she said we needed to consider our future together, and I proposed. We got married at my parent's house, the entire town was there.

We moved to Portland. We would drive out for barbecues with both of our families during the weekends. When I was practicing and traveling up to Seattle, she'd stay at my parent's house for the weeks. She got a job at some small High School, and things seemed to keep moving forward.

Then I got offered the position in Minneapolis. We moved, she followed me no questions asked. We came in May, letting the summer for the move. But then I woke up in August one day, and she was gone. She left a note. She said she couldn't do this, that she needed a life of her own, and she couldn't follow me blindly. And that the divorce papers would come.

They never came and those first few months I thought she might then come back. But then I began to get into a routine. I had Kit to make sure I did what I needed to do every week. I began to not think about Annie every day.

I thought about Kit, what Kit was doing. But whenever I did think about it, she was alone, off in her life. I never thought I was a part of it. Then I suddenly want to be a part of it. Throughout it all, I did not even really know what it was beyond the basic school and her parents and some of her friends.

It took me until about November, to get that all sorted out in my head. I spent my days cleaning, doing work, working out, teaching. I tried to keep it busy, but I let my mind process it.

I woke up on Thanksgiving with nothing to do, and I knew I needed to talk to her, before the semester was out, before she left. So I went into the student database, and looked up her address, and drove over at about 4 o'clock.

I was never this guy. The guy who pined for the girl. Who was occupied with these complexities. Everything was hunky dory until Annie left me, and it had been more than a year and this second woman had left me. But maybe I could resolve this one. I shaved my beard, put on my best blue shirt and slacks.

Her parents lived in this tiny Bungalow in St. Louis park. It was already dark but I could see the lights on. I knocked on the door, and a short (I guess compared to me) waif-like man opened the door.

"Hello, sir can I help you?"

"Hi um yes sir, Mr. Cohen, I am here to see Kit..."

"A gentleman caller for Kit? I didn't know she was expecting anyone. You name?"

"It's Jack...Jack Nyquist."

He leaned over his shoulder...and yelled "Honey, a Jack Nyquist is here for Kit."

"I don't think Kit knows anyone by that kinda name." Another woman called back.

"Why don't you ask her?" he yelled to her and turned to me "Excuse me my wife is a little fatutz over the holidays, we were expecting other guests. Do you know the Ketters, Lori, and Michael, their sons Joshua and Samuel?"

"I, ugh, no..."

"She said she knows a Jack Ny something, but she isn't expecting him." The woman yelled back...

"Well tell her he's here.""

Then the window under the front door opened and I saw her face looking down.

"I'll come down, don't worry." She yelled.

"It's almost below freezing at least chat with him inside. I'll send him up to your room."

"You don't need to do that" she called,

"Nonsense." The man said and let me in showing me up the stairs. She was standing there in the middle of the hallway.

"Hi," I said.

"Hey. Um...come in..." She led me into her room and closed the door.

"The walls aren't that thin. Or maybe my parents are ignorant of the weed." She said.

"You smoke weed," I asked.

"In High School."

Her room was painted the same light gray as my backsplash. On her, walls framed art, most photographs. A white wooden desk in a corner with a wooden bed in the center. A low dresser under the window with some pillows. I imagine her young brooding out the window onto the street. She was back in her cotton shirts and leggings. Her shoes, ballerina slippers, today. Her hair up in a bun, but she had a scarf. I guess this was doing it up for the holidays.

"Umm, take a seat." She said. I sat on her bed and she sat across from me on her bench. The sheets were a crisp white with black accents.

"I am to apologize and explain..." I said, looking down at my hands.

"Go on..." She said. So, then I told her about Annie and how she left. How I loved having her around to have someone around who was new when Annie was gone, and how I was projecting this wish for a different person onto her. A new person to be with. But that I was alone for a while, and I knew that I didn't know what I wanted, and I am sorry for using her and not telling her and for putting her on that pedestal. Before I was able to finish, she smiled. She closed her window and put her finger over her mouth as if to say, don't say anything. She unbuttoning her shirt, revealing a black bra.

"What are you doing" I whispered but she but the gesture again, Then she unbuttoned my shirt and took my pants off, folding them neatly in a corner. Then she laid her shirt and her leggings on top.

"You need to loosen up." She whispered in my ear. "Stop being so serious." She grabbed a flask from beside her bed took a swig and gave it to me. The whiskey hit the back of my throat and I took another one.

"Good you can stay for Thanksgiving dinner. She peeked opened the curtain and looked out behind me "Josh is here. With his family."

"I need to rinse up...that was..." I said and she directed me to the bathroom in her room.

We walked down the stairs where two families other than her parents were in the living area, sipping drinks.

"Honey, I'm glad you fixed it with you friend. Come now have a drink." Her dad said with a smile. She had changed into a black dress at this point and grabbed a glass of wine from him He handed one to me and said, "Don't worry it's not Maneshcvitz."

I ended up spending that first hour talking to her dad, about his work, sharing our stories. He was familiar with land rights, and was interested in what would happen for the next generation. Kit was off talking to two guys and what appeared to be their mother.

Then we sat down to a long hobbled together table for a Turkey dinner. Kit sat next to me, and we sat across from her mother and the guy Josh. Her father cut the turkey and everything was served family style.

"Kit I wish you told us earlier your friend would be joining us." Her mother sighed and then eyed Josh. Who seemed to be well-inebriated. The kid couldn't have been more than 23.

"Yeah how again did you guys meet? I feel like I know you from somewhere." I heard someone chime.

"I thought Josh was Kit's friend." The younger brother said smirking. Josh took a gulp of his drink, as Kit's mother coughed on a little food.

"Huh, Sam? Kit has a lot of friends. What's wrong with that?" The other mother said, turning to him.

"But Kit and Josh have been friends since they were fifteen." Sam continued.

"Yes and that's great I am sure Kit appreciates the friendship, but she made some new friends in college. Jack here goes to the Law School at her university." Kit's mother said, trying to move the conversation along.

"Honey, no Jack teaches at the Law School." Her father corrected her from the other end of the table, not taking a hint.

"Yeah but Josh had convinced us we needed to fly from Chicago to Minneapolis so he could see his friend."

"Yes and he is here. Aren't we all friends? Lori?" Kit's mother asked.

"Yes, I have no idea what you're saying Sam, and Josh would you like some sparkling water." Josh's mother continued.

"Wait so Jack you teach at the Law School, how do you know Kit? Must be through one of her clubs, you know we told her to get more involved" Kit's mother went on.

"Well yeah, I uh..." I started to say when the teenager, Sam, came back in.

"It's just that if Josh doesn't get to spend time with his friend he gets upset. I mean friend is a nice word cause he like loves Kit, and their friendship is special." Josh drank his glass of wine and Sam began to pour himself a cup.

"They're friends every time he comes here, in Kit's room, in the living room, at the JCC." Sam wouldn't stop.

"Sam, shut up," Lori yelled.

"Don't tell him to shut up." Josh finally spoke, looking up at Kit. Her hand was on her lap shaking as the other one held a glass of wine.

"Kit what is this, parading around some goy professor you found. You know I love you. I don't understand why you don't want to come to Georgetown Law with me." Josh said sternly.

"Kit's going to University of Washington." He father said brightly between chews. His only job was daftly interjecting with the good news, it seemed.

"Kit I feel like you need to say something, it appears you are having a lovers quarrel at the dinner table and it's making the conversation a little single sided." Her mother said sternly.

These people were officially off-beat, in my book. I was looking down at my food, but secretly I was happy. University of Washington had a great Environmental Law program.

"Thanks, Daddy, I am going to University of Washington next year, I am very sorry Josh. Also please don't use derogatory language about my friend." I wasn't really sure what was derogatory specifically, but the entire conversation seemed to be laced with innuendo that I was not picking up on.

Then he stood up and threw his napkin down. I could see his brother Sam smirking in the corner. I was not really sure what was going to happen.

"Darling, what's the fuss?" Lori said. Finally, the other man, from the other end of the table looked up and our way.

"Joshua, have you read the latest Gladwell?" He called over, before taking his glasses off to clean them with the bottom of his shirt.

"You're a bitch. You know I wasn't with anyone else when I was at Georgetown. Only during breaks, only you Kit. We took a pact that we would do everything together..." Josh began to raise his voice.

"We were fifteen..."She tried to calm him down.

"I let you..."

I suddenly let go of Kit's hand. It was getting weird.

"Sam, that is not appropriate table talk, and we discussed the pleasure centers of the prostate before it's nothing weird." What appeared to be Lori's husband said putting down his fork and knife crossing his arms.

"Wait so the two of you were sexing, and if I am to understand the implications correctly, a lot ...all over this house and other places...and Josh was expecting some sort of sex this weekend, but you are sleeping with your Professor who showed up here this afternoon to profess some thing of love to you..." Kit's mother said matter-of-factly.

"I think you have it, honey." Her father called out raising his glass for a cheers while chewing his food.

"Well Kit, I am so surprised, you seemed like such a simple girl, so mild. I am very proud that you have been exploring your options like this, but I think you may be playing with people's hearts. Josh here is really upset, and well I never took you for one to date an older man of gentile descent, but I guess you have to do it once before you settle down."

As if everything was suddenly resolved the entire table let out a little laugh went back to their stern faces.

"I think Josh needs a disco nap," Lori said.

"You can put him in the den." Her father called out. And just like that dinner resumed.

When the conversation was back, to a loud lull, Kit turned to me and said, let's go outside.

We walked into the backyard, where there was already some snow on the ground.

"I am really sorry about that. They have a very culturally unique way of expressing themselves." She said, with a blanket wrapped around her.

I pulled her close and whispered. "You're into some really...uh...deep stuff..."

"If you want to go, I understand. This is all kinda a mess."

I leaned back and shrugged "I don't see why I have to go. Unless You want me to."

"I don't. I just know I am weird...I know I am weird, and a little kinky. I didn't think you would show up here today...and yeah Josh and I, we had a lot of fun, but then you showed up, you know after months of not speaking, and it was different. You seemed open, it seemed like it can work. We don't have to get married, we can just date and be together"

"So let's try to make it work. Let's date and be together." I said and I hugged her close and we went back inside.

2.5

Kit

I guess I had never really dated anyone before, in the open. Those six months between when I finished school in December and when I moved to Washington were a whirlwind.

In my head, and on paper, it was odd dating a former professor who still had a marriage. He said he was going to begin the divorce papers it in the fall after. It had been a full two years since Annie left. It didn't bother me. I didn't think I was going to marry the guy or anything. I was still young.

I got a job as a receptionist at a local law firm in St. Paul. I would go to work in the morning and come home. I think it was an adjustment for Jack as well. In December he came to one night of Hanukkah, and Chinese Dinner on Christmas. I didn't really introduce him to Soshi and Tova when they were back, but when they left we spent time with this guy Jeff who knew his brother. At first, I didn't mind the long afternoons, and sleeping in my own bed at my parents.

Then I got that receptionist job. And we'd both be home exhausted. I spent a few nights in his guest room until I finally asked about it.

He said he felt bad because he hadn't really even gotten new sheets since Annie left. So one day I asked if I could go in and redecorate. He said sure. The room was boring, but sentimental, pictures of his family on the dresser. We went to a store and got new sheets and broke them that afternoon.

He liked coming over and talking to my dad on Sunday afternoons when he would drop me off. They'd swap stories or ideas. For his 32nd birthday, we went to Stillwater for the weekend. I guess it doubled as a romantic Valentine's day.

The sex was, it was getting better. One afternoon in a dark February on his living room floor, I told him I would explain the anatomy to him.

"I guess they don't teach you this in Lumberjack school." I teased him.

"No they didn't missy, so teach away, but I gotta warn you, you may not get far in this lesson" I started.

That was winter.

2.6

Jack

The girl was fun. Winter was nice. It was good to be around the sort of people who did not take themselves so seriously. Her father used to say, in this shrugging way "We all got problems."

She would stay the night once or twice a week, but when school started I would ask her to sleep over most nights, she would decline about half of them. Like she was keeping some distance.

The spring courses were going, well. Jase said he had met someone and was really happy. He said he had things under control in Astoria. The rain came in April and we'd walk outside in the cold and come home to make sweet sex while we warmed up. It was different from being with Annie cause Kit liked to tease me, but in the end, it was all about pleasure. There was no score, nothing to prove. Some days she'd leave and I'd go to bed having to rub one out thinking about the afternoon.

She made me try new things. Not that I was averse to trying new things, I just never had a reason to before. May came, and I got a summer position again. That's when we finally started to talk about her move. She was going to get an apartment, somewhere cheap, needed some recommendations. I said I'd call around. Her father announced that he and her mother were moving back to New York after she moved. He got a position at Cornell, wanted to be back with family.

I told her I'd visit her on weekend. She asked how I could afford it. I told her not to worry. I'd figure it out. She said we didn't need to stay together, but I wanted to. I really wanted to, cause she made me happy. I wanted to show her things, tell her things.

I think I had that with Annie, but it was something different. With Annie it was like I was lucky to be with her. She was a belle and I needed to constantly show her how we could be happy.

I found her a studio apartment on the top of a house on the backside of a neighborhood called Capitol Hill, close to the school. She and I would drive the pickup and her parents would fly out to meet us.

It was a week before we left that I got a call from Jase. He said that if I could soon, to come by the house. Something about Pops, some tests, his health. Just wanted to check in.

The drive was beautiful. The air was clear and we combed in and out of Dakotas to Montana. We took our sweet time, combing through the thinnest part of Idaho, to the great flats to the Cascades.

I didn't tell her that I was gonna go down south after she was unpacked. Didn't want to bother her.

We spent a week together in Seattle. I showed her around some my old favorite places. We christened the apartment. Then when she was unpacked and in, I started the drive to Long View.

When I got to the house, which was on a hill outside of Astoria, my brother was there waving with my dad. This was the formal welcome everyone got, friend or family.

I opened the door, stepped out. Jase gave me a barrel hug. Then Pops.
"It's nothing just Melanoma, already been removed, don't know why Jase brought ya down here."

"Dad you know why," Jase said back. I didn't even know about the cancer. I had spoken to my dad every now and again on the phone, but it was always about what parcel of land they were working that month, or what my mom had made for dinner.

"We're gonna finish this up and the plans in place," I said patting him on the back.

From the hill, you could see a faint glimmer of the Columbia River and a forest all around. In the back distance, the large column in Astoria climbed high on a clear day.

I laid in my childhood bed. Jase said he was staying at his house down the ways. The house was quiet that you could still hear my Pop's snores.

It was the next morning that things got rough. After breakfast Jase came by and said he wanted me to come over, wanted to show me something.

He lived in the same size house just two miles down the road on another hill. We walked and I could hear a baby crying and a voice.

"Jase that you."

I knew that voice. That was the voice I had been waiting to call me. To say, here we're done, let's sign it.

I began to back away from the door.

"No, I have to explain something to you, Jack. I need this to come out, come clean."

"Jase," Annie called again, before coming through the living area. She was carrying a baby who was now soothed, sucking on a toy. She looked good. Her hair in a perfect ponytail. Her jeans snugly fitted. Her makeup on her face so intently. She looked like Annie, and nothing had ever happened to her.

She looked at me and went silent.

"I need to put the baby down." She announced, and then walked over to a play pen.

"What is going on here? Whose baby is that?" I sputtered, my voice cracking like a kids. I began to clench my hands in my pockets.

"It's Jase's, don't worry Jack," Annie said coming forward and closing her arms.

"Jase you got Annie taking care of your kid?" I could feel my crackling growing. I didn't want to know the arrangement. I just wanted to leave. But Jase held my arm and looked me in the eye, his face contorted in some mess.

"It's Annie's kid too." He said.

I looked up at him silently then over to her. Her arms were wrapped around her chest, and her face was also concerned.

"Jack I need you to grant Annie a divorce, so we can get married," Jase said trying to stay calm.

"Grant Annie a divorce? Hell, I would have gave her one months ago if I knew where she was. Turns out she was here all along."

"She needed a place to come." He said trying to explain.

"What do you mean? Annie has this been going on since you left me?"

"No, no that's not what happened Jack."

"Annie tell him." Jase pleaded with her.

"Jack, do you wanna take a seat." She said.

"Not really, till you can explain to me what is happening here. Cause this seems like some trashy shit."

"Jack, I ran into Jase that February after I left... in Portland. I was living with a friend and he said you had moved on. You'd met someone in Minneapolis....You know how much I've always loved your brother."

"Loved my brother?" I said, hushly. I couldn't understand. Annie was always giving herself to me, trying to get me to want her. Through high school, through our time in Seattle. She explained that Jase offered her a room in his house, cause he felt bad since it seemed like I had built this new life. He said he understood how she didn't wanna leave her family and her home for Minneapolis. She said she always had feelings for Jase. That she would be around me to see him, and it just happened that we got together. That we went too far down our path together. But then it happened, they started spending time together, one thing led to another. I tried to listen calmly. To not be the brute. I just looked down and listened, rubbing my chin and combing my hair to keep my hands occupied.

She was gonna contact me and get the divorce. Then she had gotten pregnant and my dad had gotten sick. Things just got busy. But they were getting less busy and now seemed like a good time

"I understand what you are all saying, and I will consider my options here and get back to you." I said simply, and walked down the driveway to my car.

I got back in the driver's seat, headed to my parents and packed my stuff, and drove back to Minneapolis alone.

Part 3

3.1

Kit

Seattle was this new place. For the first few days it was light for hours, from four a.m. till ten p.m, then suddenly it became dark. Then a moody, alcohol infused din fell over the city. At first it was cold, but then I felt warm. My apartment was on the curly end of 13th avenue and Aloha. In a quiet complex that looked like a Tudor castle. It was like a secret block in the middle of the city. I'd take the bus down to campus every day, picking up a coffee along the way. Looking back, it was just another city in pine trees along the north-westward way, and yet it pleased me, entirely.

I kept my head down at school, waiting for long breaks and weekends. For Jack to come. And he did, any weekend he could, he'd fly or drive, and we'd spend the weekends wandering in all the secret neighborhoods around the city. For Thanksgiving, we cooked a chicken in my tiny oven. That year had passed like a day into night.

We were laying in bed when he asked what I wanted to do for winter break. I said I wasn't sure, I didn't have a lot of money to travel. I didn't want to go back to Minneapolis. My parents were coming for a few days around Christmas, but other than that it was free.

Jack came up, and we went out for Chinese food in the I.D., and then he stayed for three weeks. And for three weeks we played real house. Buying groceries for more than a night, seeing movies, making plans. And then Jase showed up.

3.2

Jack

It was a week before the term started when I told the school I had a family emergency and needed to head home. I found an apartment in Portland pretty quickly. I didn't tell Jase or Annie at first, and I didn't tell Kit. I needed to get this resolved before I got her into this mess.

It was a large studio in the Pearl District. I hired some company to send my stuff from Minneapolis and put it in storage. Kit wasn't going back there anytime soon, and I was alone in the world. Didn't seem worth keeping it all on hand.

I called Jase and told him that I was in Portland for a while and that we'd solve this. I was mad at him alright. But I knew that the company would be split 50/50 between us, and if we wanted to keep things in operations for another hundred years we'd need to get along decent.

I was mad at Annie. I was mad at Annie for sure. She strung me along all these years. But looking back I could see it. She always wanted me to be more like my brother. To be the lumbering type. She used to say I was such a bookworm and I needed to work with my hands more.

I began to take on small contract work as the divorce proceedings began. On the weekends I could get free, I'd head up to Seattle by train. Kit never asked any questions, she seemed preoccupied with school, and her new city. It was like I was taking short breaks, from the reality of my fucked up family. The whole story seemed to trashy whenever I thought about it. But when the divorce was done, I could package it to her, and it would work.

I started the paperwork for the divorce, but it was a slow roll. Jase would come up sometimes and we'd talk about the business. Never about Annie. We'd buyout my father, give him a good retirement. Manage it 50/50. He'd be on the operations side, and I the administration. The thing was, I don't think I even wanted to do that. I wanted to get back to teaching, but we all have our obligations.

I planned to fake a winter break and spend the three weeks up in Seattle. We were about two weeks in, when I got a call one morning.

"Brother, we need to talk."

"Jase, what is it?"

"I am in Seattle."

"Fuck, what do you need now." Kit rolled over and looked up at me as I sat up. She rested her head in my lap.

"Where are you?" He asked through the phone.

"At Kit's."

"Come meet me at the Elysian at noon." He said and hung up.

"Everything okay?" Kit asked.

"Jase is in Seattle," I replied.

"Well, that's nice of him to come up. " She replied, getting out of bed. She slinked over to the bathroom, naked, and turned on the shower.

"He wants to meet at the Elysian at noon."

She stepped into the shower and saying nothing.

"You want to come?" I called to her. I don't know why I asked. I think I thought, well if she's there Jase can't pull more crazy on me. He's gotta be good. Right?

And so we made the long walk down thirteenth avenue in the dark mist and green trees. We sat the bar and waited for Jase. He was a few minutes late but greeted me with a handshake leading into a hug. Kit got a kiss on the cheek.

He didn't sit down before he started in "Annie needs her divorce."

I placed my beer down and looked at him.

"The paperwork is almost ready."

"Well let's move it along, brother."

"When break is done, first thing."

"Okay, I believe you," Jase said reassuringly. Kit sat quietly listening on, looking down the bar.

"Wanna grab a cigarette," Jase said. I didn't smoke, and I knew he didn't but I nodded and went outside with him. It was feeling dark, and within a few seconds of being outside a dampness already covered us

"Annie's pregnant again, and it's only gonna get more complicated."

"I'll be in Portland next week, back home. You two come over and we'll have this done."

When I looked over, Kit was outside. We moved onto the next bar.

3.3

Kit

I pretended like I hadn't heard him mention Portland or any of the conversations because I didn't really know what to do right then and there. But when Jase left and we came home, I began to think.

I knew the divorce was pending, but *pregnant again* seemed to imply there was more going on. *And I'll be in Portland next week, back home. You two come over.*

The last week Jack was there felt like a blur, because I kept trying to sneak moments to go through his things, to see what was really happening. All I found was a key that wasn't to his house in Minneapolis, and some texts with his brother about their family's business.

Then he left, and I went back to school. He wasn't planning to come back to Seattle until February. But that first weekend alone, I don't know…I rented a car one Friday night and began to drive down to Astoria.

I did not even know where to look for him. I stayed a crappy hotel and the next morning headed out around the town. It sounded like a small enough place,, where I could convince someone to tell me about his whereabouts.

It didn't take me long to simply see Jase standing in front of a house, cleaning some gutters. I pulled into the driveway and parked. I was taking a moment, to collect myself, figure out my next move, when I looked up and he was at my window. He knocked on it.

"You know round here, it's impolite to show up places without calling." He smiled.

"We need to stop meeting like this, in cars..." I tried to sound witty. He came around the side and passenger seat.

"What can I do for you today Kit."

"Ya gonna invite me in?" I asked.

"No."

I looked at him.

"This isn't my house, ya see. It's Annie's. You know who that is?"

"Yes."

"Now I know you're smart, gonna be a lawyer and all, and so I don't want to have to explain something to her that doesn't need explaining, a random girl showing up and stuff. Not even gonna ask how you found me. Just wondering what your looking for..."

"I am looking for Jack."

"Let's switch seats." He said. I looked at him again, not sure whether to trust him.

"Girl, get in the passenger seat here. Let's go for a drive." He continued, getting out. I shifted over to the passenger side, and he got in.

"This is one tiny car." He exclaimed adjusting the seat, before starting the ignition.

We headed off down the road I was driving on, back into town.

"You know they filmed Goonies here..." He said trying to make polite conversation. I just stared out the window to the houses, which all seemed to get older as we drove farther into the town, and be propped up by the wind.

"I don't like getting mixed up in my brother's business." He said.

"I'm not here to cause trouble...I just."

"No I know you're not, you just care about him and you figured something out, I dunno what."

"I mean....I thought we were going somewhere, the two of us. But maybe we're not. Maybe that's why he has this whole other life I don't know about..."

"I mean I don't know. I don't want to put ideas in your head or anything, but regardless of where you two are going, you came a long way from somewhere, and he needs to be straight with you."

"Do you think I love him?" I asked him, without any hesitation.

Jase paused for a moment and said, "I think you want to."

"I really want to," I replied.

We pulled up to a tower cover it artwork that looked out into a gray sea.

"This is a good place to think....take in some perspective and what not....Listen...I want him to be happy you know. I didn't mean for this all to happen. And when he found you, it seemed like he had moved forward, moved on. But then he moved to Portland. Portland's damn close. " Jase meandered through his thoughts.

"You seem very talkative today. I never thought of you as the talkative one."

"I feel like I owe you something, Kit. Now listen, I am not starting something, but, whatever this means to you. Maybe he's in Portland to be closer to you."

"I didn't even know he was in Portland." I replied.

"Well he was, but the divorce is over, this week officially. Papers signed."

"What does that mean for you?" I asked.

"I've always loved Annie. Jack, he had to learn to love her and he did. I always loved her and I didn't know it until I did. And you see Annie and I, we went the same things. We're having our second kid you, know. And I love it, I love being with her, she is there for me. Cooks me dinner every night. Gives me what I want. She's a woman, though, a complicated creature, like you. She feels bad about this whole thing I think...even if she doesn't, I think she's resolute. It's all settled. It's all settled between us."

"And with Jack?"

"Well, we're buying out my dad, and taking ownership in the Spring...I dunno if Jack will ever be settled. But Kit, you focus on your school and being good at whatever it is you want to do. Don't get tied up in our mess, go create your own."

He took out his wallet, and a pen and began to write on a piece of paper.

"Here's his address in Portland."

When I got there, it was dark. All you could see was a sprinkle of small city lights and a flickering along the river. His building was a converted loft space somewhere hip. I didn't wanna buzz him, so I waited outside until someone let me slip in. Then I walked up to his unit, on the top floor, avoiding the elevators. I needed to struggle, it couldn't be this easy.

I knocked on the door.

"Who is it." I heard from behind the door.

"Hey," I said back. I could feel him looking through the peephole.

The door swung open. He was standing naked, there holding a towel up. His beard had grown back in, dark. His brow was furrowed.

I walked in and he dropped the towel. He walked over and pulled me in, kissing me.

3.4

Jack

She stood naked staring out into the dark Portland night, from the floor the ceiling windows. You could see the little buildings towering, making a skyline. Like Portland was a real place. Like this was all happening.

The apartment was sparse. A white bed, and kitchenette in the corner, some shelves with baskets as clothes a desk on one side.

"So this is it. This is where you live now?" She said calmly.

I sat up on the bed, putting my arms on my knees, she turned around.

"I missed the beard. I like you in it."

I looked at my palms, trying to see if the wrinkles would come together to tell me what to do next. They call it a lifeline, and I needed it. I knew what was gonna happen. I didn't know when, but I knew soon, soon I would be alone again.

"We are like two atoms, who hit each other, changing each other's course." She went over to my kitchenette and began to grab a bottle of wine. In the darkness, in her movements, it felt like she had grown infinitely. Moved infinitely away from me. I began to think back to the years before, trying to see if that would give me something...

"You know, I've never really had my heart broken before. I've been hurt." She plunged a corkscrew into the top and began to twist. With one quick jolt, she pulled the cork out. She poured only one glass, for herself and took a sip.

"I'm not trying to hurt you Kit....how did you even..."

"I know, you're a broken man...I found your brother first, actually. You know there are a lot of broken men out there. It's not really an excuse. Anyhow your brother..." She took a deep sip, "You know what he asked me? He asked me if I thought you loved me..."

"Kit, I love you."

"No, I think you want to love me. I think I represent something you want, some other life. But it's like you can't let go of the past. And I want to love you. But why are you even here? The divorce is done, I know. You don't need to be here to do admin work for the business...Go back to Minneapolis. Go somewhere...Go live your life."

"You're being critical."

She took another sip of wine.

"You're right." She said simply and then came back into the bed. I pulled the glass out of her hand and finished the last of it. I walked over to the kitchenette, got the bottle and came back to the bed. We drank.

In the morning, she was gone and I shaved my beard.

www.ingramcontent.com/pod-product-compliance
Lightning Source LLC
Chambersburg PA
CBHW070646130626
46555CB00006B/2725